COLLEGE SEX TALES

EXPLICIT DIRTY EROTICA SHORT STORIES

SAGE YARBER

plicit Press
Erotica Fiction

CHAPTER 1

CHECKOUT TIME

TWENTY-THREE-YEAR-OLD AUBREY MADISON had been watching the twenty-one-year-old for several weeks. She'd even spoken to him a few times as she'd checked out his books and was sure he found her attractive too. Just what it was preventing Nicco Greene from asking her out like so many other students, she didn't know. With the end of the finals approaching and graduation looming, tonight was her last chance and she'd decided to go all out.

She'd left her golden blond curls down around her shoulders and applied a pale purple eye shadow that complemented her light violet eyes. Instead of her normal sensible black skirt and a white blouse, she'd taken advantage of the nice spring weather and worn a dark purple halter top and shorter, tighter skirt, sans pantyhose. A bold approach wasn't usually her style, but she was desperate. It had been almost a year since she'd last gotten laid and her self-induced orgasms were no longer as satisfying as they had once been.

It was close to midnight before Nicco arrived. His

copper curls were damp. A hot flare of desire sparked in her belly and solidified her decision.

She watched him walk away. She was unable to take her eyes off his lean swimmer's body. His sweatpants and t-shirt just accentuated the muscles he'd built up becoming the school's fastest freestyler. She couldn't wait to see if the cock underneath those pants matched the fantasies she'd had playing out in her head ever since she'd seen a picture of him in those tiny swim trunks.

Aubrey glanced up at the clock. She'd give him a couple of minutes to get settled in before she headed back to the small alcove Nicco frequented. While she waited, she reached under her skirt and shimmied out of her panties. Might as well speed things along. She doubted anyone would notice her absence, but even as eager as she was, she wasn't about to risk her job. She put up her sign and took a deep breath. It was time.

He was exactly where she'd thought he'd be: sitting in one of the plush chairs, head bent over a book. Shadows played across his face as he turned the pages. As she approached, he looked up. "Something wrong?" The confusion on his face turned to shock as Aubrey reached behind her

to untie the top of her halter.

"Aubrey?" The book fell to the ground, unnoticed.

She smiled and let her top fall around her waist, exposing her firm breasts to the cool library air.

.   .   .

Her tan nipples hardened almost immediately. Nicco's eyes were wide, darkening with lust as Aubrey walked over to his chair, stopping when she was straddling his legs.

As she reached down to cup his burgeoning erection, she spoke. "No strings. No drama. I just want this," she gave him a gentle squeeze, "inside me."

Nicco swallowed hard and nodded.

Aubrey's smile grew as she tugged Nicco's sweats down to free his now rock-hard cock. It was as nice as she'd imagined. She ran her hand over the impressive length and Nicco groaned, hips involuntarily jerking. Her free hand shook with anticipation as she drew a small packet from the waistband of her skirt. She tore it open with her teeth; eyes on Nicco as she reached down to roll it over his dick.

"Fuck," the word came out in a shuddered breath.

"Exactly," Aubrey moaned as she sank down on him, letting him fill her inch by exquisite inch. "Oh, fuck," Nicco's fingers flexed against Aubrey's hips as she came to rest on his lap.

Aubrey made a small sound of satisfaction. This was what she'd been craving. The feeling of fullness and connection that she couldn't get from her own hand or a toy. No matter how quickly she could bring herself off it just wasn't the same. She reached down and took his hands in hers. Gazes locked, she moved his hands to her breasts.

Nicco took the hint. His fingers caressed her flesh and teased her nipples. As she began to move, he leaned forward, wrapping his lips around one of her hardened nubs. Aubrey tossed her head back, flexing her hips as she rocked back and forth.

"I'm not going to last long," Nicco released her nipple long enough to warn her.

Aubrey nodded, increasing her pace. Her lithe body danced on top of his. She could feel it building, the pressure that promised ultimate relief, the answer to the ache inside her. Nicco had returned his attention to her breasts, teeth scraping over sensitive flesh before laving his tongue over the newly pink area. His hands slid over her back, one splaying at the base, the other moving to her neck. His fingers dug into her curls. When he yanked on them to give him better access to her breasts, Aubrey cried out. The sound drew a growl from Nicco and he bit down on her breast.

"Shit," Aubrey's body shook as she climaxed. Her muscles spasmed around Nicco, sending him spiraling over the edge, calling out her name as he came. The sensation of him pulsing inside her as he filled the condom sent another ripple of pleasure through her and she fell forward. As she rested against his chest, her over-sensitive nipples rubbed against his shirt and her body shuddered with an aftershock.

"May I ask," Nicco's voice was breathless, his hands making small circles on her bareback. "What prompted that?"

Aubrey pushed herself backward and stood legs still shaky. As she re-tied her top, Nicco pulled off the condom and tucked himself back into his pants. "I've been waiting all semester for you to make a move. You didn't, so I figured tonight was as good a night as any."

Before he could ask her out or make any awkward

inquiries about when he could see her again, she started to walk away, not pausing as she called over her shoulder, "Thanks."

It wasn't until she got home that she realized she'd left her panties on the floor behind the library counter.

CHAPTER 2

THE DIFFICULT PROFESSOR

SHAYE FRYE KNEW she was going to fail her Intro to Theater class. She hated acting, had stage fright actually, and had only taken the class because she was two credits short of being a full-time student. It was either that or a physical education class. And the only thing she hated worse than acting was Phys. Ed. So, now she had to go to her professor's office to ask for extra credit or she was going to lose her scholarship.

Had the circumstances been different, Shaye would've been pleased to go see the hottest professor on campus. At twenty-eight, he was only nine years older than Shaye and was fuckably hot. Shaggy Sienna's hair made him look more like a student than a member of the faculty and his chocolate brown eyes were always warm. As she headed down the hallway to his office, Shaye had to admit that he'd been the star of several of her masturbatory fantasies. When he called for her to come in, she tossed her shoulder-length light brown hair over her shoulder, fixed what she hoped was a contrite expression on her face, and opened the door.

"Miss Frye," the professor's voice sent a shiver through

Shaye that had nothing to do with temperature. "How can I help you?"

Shaye's blue-green eyes ran over the professor's lean body and she took a moment to wonder as she always did, what was hidden beneath his stylish suits. She decided that straightforward was the best policy. "I was wondering if there were any extra credit assignments I could do to get my grade up."

Professor Underhill studied her for a moment before reaching into his desk and producing a folder. He handed it over without changing his expression. "In the folder, you will find the role you are to play during class tomorrow. Do well and I'll replace one of your poor grades with a better one."

On her way to class the next morning, Shaye could feel her cheeks burning. The character she'd been given wasn't what she'd expected, but she'd dutifully memorized all of the provided information and had even followed her character's dress code to the letter. Her tall, athletic body usually clothed in jeans and comfy hoodies was currently wearing a short skirt that barely covered her ass, a peasant top and five-inch heels. This had been bad enough, but the inclusion of the character's choices for undergarments – no bra and a red thong – had been the icing on the cake, so to speak. She'd never been so thankful for her relatively small breasts.

When she reached class, a few minutes late thanks to her new outfit, Professor Underhill waved her down to a seat at the front of the room. Remembering her character's innate desire to please authority figures, Shaye bit back a snarky comment and did as she was told. She couldn't help flashing a little panty as she crossed her legs. The professor's eyes widened for a moment and then returned his attention to the rest of the class.

As the class wore on, Shaye found herself teasing the professor more and more. She'd shift in her seat, flashing the rapidly dampening crotch of her red thong, or she'd lean forward, letting the loose neck of her shirt slip down to reveal the tops of her breasts. He never faltered in his lesson, the only indications that her actions were affecting him was the darkening of his eyes and his subtle movement to stand behind his desk for the final twenty minutes of the session.

"Be sure to read the next two essays for Monday's class," Professor Underhill's gaze flicked to Shaye. "And, Miss Frye, if I could see you for a moment."

Shaye walked up to the desk, stomach in knots. If he didn't think she'd done well enough for at least a B, she was screwed. When he turned from watching the last of the students leave, however, she knew she'd done well. The professor's hand dropped to the large bulge in the front of his pants, lazily rubbing as he walked towards her.

"You were quite the tease today, Miss Frye," his voice caressed her skin, liquid warmth that made her pussy drip. "And I think you need to do something about that."

She didn't stop to think about what she should do. She just knew what her character would do.

She dropped to her knees in front of the professor and looked up at him through her lashes. A smile flashed across his face and he unzipped his pants as he crossed the last few feet to stand in front of her. "Show me your tits."

. . .

Somehow, the word seemed more vulgar in his cultured voice.

Shaye yanked on the front of her shirt, exposing her firm breasts. The pale rose-colored nipples were already hard and she ran her fingers over them, smiling at the groan that fell from her professor's lips. She slid her index finger into her mouth hollowing her cheeks as she sucked on it.

"I think I have something better for that mouth of yours," he shoved his pants and boxers below his hips, revealing a long, thick cock that curved up towards what looked like washboard abs.

Shaye reached for the swollen shaft, all thoughts of her character falling away. All she knew now was that she wanted that beautiful piece of flesh in her mouth. She wrapped her lips around the head, letting her tongue swirl around it. Using the tip of her tongue, she teased his slit, hearing him swear as she licked the salty pre-cum, letting the taste of him coat her tongue. She ran the flat of her tongue up the underside of his cock before engulfing his length in one swift motion.

"Shit," the professor buried his hand in her hair, fisting the locks in a near-painful grip.

Her hand made its way beneath her skirt as she began to move her head, letting the velvet steel in her mouth slide over her tongue, and bump against the back of her throat. She moaned around his cock as she slipped two fingers into her wet core.

"Make yourself cum," Professor Underhill tightened his grip on her hair, and she cried out, the sound muffled by his dick. He began to move her head and she let him, relinquishing control little by little until she had none. She sheathed her teeth and concentrated on her breathing, her fingers working themselves into her cunt and over her clit. He forced himself deeper and she nearly gagged. "I won't stop until you make yourself cum."

Shaye could feel the pressure building inside her, hot lava bubbling in her stomach, wanting nothing more than to spill out over her skin and take her into ecstasy. She shoved a third finger into her pussy and shuddered. So close. She whimpered, riding an edge that threatened to drive her mad. She dropped the hand that had been resting on his hip and grabbed one of her breasts, tugging at her nipple. She was barely aware that the professor was fucking her face even faster, the tip of him sliding down into her throat on every other stroke.

"Cum!"

It was an order this time and Shaye felt the power of it ripple over her. Her body stiffened as she came, swallowing instinctively, neck muscles working around the head of his cock.

"Fuck," he growled as he went rigid, emptying himself down her throat.

He held her head against him, her face pressed against his pelvis until she tried to pull away. He kept her there just a few seconds longer before releasing her and Shaye sat back, panting as she tried to get air back into her burning lungs. She swallowed her throat on fire.

"So, Professor," her voice sounded raspy. "How did I do?"

Professor Underhill tucked himself back into his pants, hands a little unsteady. "I think you really personified your character. That should get you a passing grade." He picked up his briefcase. "But if you're interested in getting up to a C, I have a few other characters you could try out."

Shaye's eyes stayed fixed on the professor's tight ass as he walked out of the classroom. A higher grade would help her GPA, she told herself as she got to her feet. It certainly had nothing to do with her desire to feel her professor's cock in her pussy. Shaye adjusted her thong. Nothing at all.

CHAPTER 3

COLLEGE SPRING BREAK SEX PARTY

HEATHER AND ANNA were the best of friends. They had been best friends since Junior High and had made a pact that they would attend the same college together. Many people thought that they were lesbians, due to the fact that they seemed almost unable to be separated from one another. They were just super close friends. They had even lost their virginity together on the same night to a couple of brothers they picked up at the local movie theater.

They decided that they were going to head to Daytona for Spring Break. This was one of the most exciting times of the year and often they spent their time off from school going on boring trips with their respective parents. This was their first chance to do something together. They made the arrangements and headed out as soon as the last class had let out. They arrived at the hotel and decided to go for dinner. They had heard about this restaurant that was famous for its French Toast. Anna was allergic to eggs, so she asked that hers be made with egg substitutes. When the orders arrived both girls dove into their food with Anna thinking nothing about it. After dinner, they headed back to their room. They were planning on grabbing a couple of hours of sleep before heading out to party on the town.

Anna was in the bathroom shortly after they got back, very sick to her stomach. The hotel had an in-house doctor that Heather called for her friend. After a few minutes, the doctor showed up and Heather, as upset as she was, forgot that she was topless and answered the door. The doctor looked at Heather.

Finally, Heather took the doctor to Anna. The doctor gave her a shot and told Anna to go lie down for a few minutes to let the shot work. Heather was very grateful for what had been done and told the doctor that she was willing to do anything to show her gratitude. Heather played with her nipples in an attempt to get the doctor aroused and interested in having sex with her.

The doctor came over to Heather and leaned down to begin nursing on her nipples. The one thing that Heather failed to tell most men that she was with was that she could naturally lactate without being pregnant. Her body produced breast milk just the same as though she was pregnant. The doctor was nursing on the nipple when a shot of milk shot out of her nipple and into the mouth of the doctor.

Being taken by surprise for a second, he jerked back only to regain his composure rather quickly. The man went back to the task at hand.

He took a couple of fingers and inserted them into the wet cunt of Heather. Making a motion that allowed the tips of his fingers to rub her clit, Heather was having an immense amount of pleasure. The doctor knew all of the spots to hit that would drive Heather into a frenzy and knew that soon she would be gushing juices at an uncontrollable pace. Heather reached down and undid the zipper of the pants that the doctor was wearing. Heather was able to feel the rigid outline of the larger-than-average cock that was inside his boxers. Heather pulled the cock out and began to slowly and gently rub it up and down in a rather gentle motion.

The doctor responded with the flow of precum that sprang from the end of his knob. Heather moved closer and pulled her panties to one side. This allowed the doctor the best access to her snatch that any other position could have afforded him. The end of his knob slid across the opening of her pussy and allowed him the chance to send electrical currents shooting through her body. It had been a while since any man had been that forward with her and had even come close to giving her the pleasure that she had been seeking. The continued thrusting in and out was driving her to the point of madness and was pushing her to a point that she needed to be at. It was a long time and she needed a good fucking to unleash all of the sexual energy that was built up inside of her.

The motions continued for what seemed forever until both her and the doctor were getting to the point that they were about to unleash a torrent of passion juices. Heather had backed things off a little and was trying to make things last as long as she could, as the sensation of a good fucking was driving her to the point of wanting to let loose there on the spot. Another reason that she didn't want to orgasm was that she was trying to hold out and allow Anna the chance for her to finish herself off. Anna had at this point recovered enough that she was able to begin working her cunt over while watching her best friend and the man that saved her life have wild, unbridled sex in front of her.

The rest of Spring break was spent a lot like the first night. It was the perfect vacation for the two best friends.

CHAPTER 4

EXTRA CREDIT

I AM a college student and I attend one of the biggest universities in the country. I took my life as a student very seriously, but this particular semester I was having problems with a difficult trigonometry class. I didn't take my grades lightly so I set up an appointment to see the professor in his office so we could discuss my grade and my issues with his class. I was due to see him in his private office in 10 minutes so I raced across campus to the building where his office was as quickly as I could.

I made it to his office right in the nick of time and I rapped lightly on his door. He told me to come in so I entered inside the office kind of shyly. He was an amazingly smart man and incredibly handsome too. That added to my nerves. I had a secret crush on him and I had ever since the semester started. Older men have always made my pussy wet, and he fits the bill perfectly. He was tall, silver-headed, and he wore wire-frame glasses that made him look as intelligent as he deserved to.

I sat down across from him and remembered I had worn my tank top that showed off my ample tits and my belly with my belly button ring. I could have sworn I noticed the professor looking at my pointed nipples through my top. The thought of him wanting me filled me with ecstasy but I tried to keep my mind on the matter at hand. We talked a bit about my grades and my issues with the class. He offered me some worksheets so that I could achieve extra credit to bring my grades up. I agreed of course.

I was getting up ready to leave when I noticed the top of the professor's arm moving like he was doing something under the top of his desk. At first, I was a bit taken aback.

Surely he wasn't doing what it looked like he was doing. The sheer thought of it made my pussy get drenched in two seconds flat. The professor looked at me and asked me what was wrong that I looked like I had seen a ghost. I stammered an unintelligible reply.

He stood up at that time and revealed his hard erection to me standing straight out from his zipper. "Do you like what you see Miss Thompson?" he asked sexily. I was in shock but I replied, "Of course I do. I am just surprised that's all." "I have seen you in class. I have seen you show me your pretty pussy under your tiny mini-skirts, Miss Thompson. I know you want a taste of my cock and don't deny it." "I won't deny it," I replied.

Professor Whitlock walked toward me and started to rub the length of his shaft over my hand. Without thinking, I started to jerk on it. He was getting me incredibly horny and I knew I was going to fuck him before I left his office.

I dropped to my knees and spread my legs in a squatted position so he could see my furry muff smile up at him while I sucked his bulging dick. He groaned in obvious plea-sure as I toyed with the head of his cock, running circles around it with my tongue's tip. I fingered my clit while I sucked and licked his raging boner. He told me to climb up on his desk and get in the doggie position. I thought he was going to immediately start banging me but much to my surprise he first lapped on my cunt lips. It felt fucking amaz-ing. I had never had it licked and lapped so proficiently. I stuck my ass straight up in the air and pushed my cunt out to meet his mouth as far as I could get it to stick out. I could tell he was enjoying it because he began to rub his whole face all over my starving pussy. When he did that, it made me start to rub it all over him ferociously. I was getting so horny I started to scream, wanting to squirt all over the professor.

'I've always wanted to fuck your horny cunt, Miss Thompson." He said and that made me want to squirt immediately. He plunged his hard tongue in me and tongue fucked me right to the point of orgasm. I fucked him back with deep thrusts to his mouth. He suddenly stopped and went to sit down in his leather office chair. He motioned for me to come over and sit down on his raging hard-on and of course, I did. He grabbed me gently around the waist and guided me one inch at a time onto his throbbing meat. After the first few inches made their way inside of me, I began to squirm uncontrollably, wanting the rest of it buried inside of me. It was so long and fat that it filled me to perfection. It was the best dick I had ever had inside of my wet cunt.

Finally, he buried every last inch inside of me and I began to ride his cock like a cowgirl. I moved on it every which way I could and then some. He held my hips as I'd rise up to the very end of his head and then slam back down onto his cock nearly burying him balls deep inside of me.

He grabbed my ponytail and pulled back as I sat straight up on his throbbing prick. With each release and each thrust, the two of us got closer to an orgasm. He'd suck my hard nipples while I squirmed and grinded on top of him. His face sort of clenched up and I knew my professor was about to shoot the fuck off. He pushed me hard down on him, and I felt my lips wrap tight around his shaft. I felt pressure and his balls draw up. At the same precise moment, he and I had an explosive orgasm that dripped erotically onto his brown leather chair. We both screamed like horny and hungry animals as we released our seed. It just goes to show that getting a little extra credit after class sometimes pays off. It did for me in a big way. It continued for the remainder of the semester as well.

CHAPTER 5

GETTING THE PASSING GRADE

MOLLY SIMS WAS a daddy's girl, anything that she wanted, she got. Money was not an object. If she could not buy it with money, she used sex. This was how she spent her high school years and she did not see a need to stop now that she was in college.

She tried to buy a few of her professors off and there were a couple that went along with it. Then there was Mr. Harris. Money was not going to buy his good grades. She was told that she would have to come to his class on a daily basis and take her tests and pass them on her own. Molly was not deterred. She was determined that one way or another she was going to get to him and buy his favor. She went to the first couple of classes and noticed that Mr. Harris seemed to have an interest in her and her revealing outfits. Molly felt that she had found a way to this old man's heart. Molly was not excited about the potential of sucking him off on a regular basis, but it was better than failing. Molly went up to him one day after class and set an appointment to meet with him to discuss her grades and the potential of doing extra credit. He told her to be in his office the next day at 3:00.

The next day as she was told to do. She was at his office on time. He told her to come in and have a seat. Molly found it odd that he was acting as if he was actually going to talk to her about this. Molly was told that she had a choice, she could write an in-depth report on the social impact of war on the economy or she could put out for her grades. Molly knew immediately that the only way that she was going to get the grades she needed without doing the work herself was going to be on her knees in one way or another. She sat there and listened to what the professor was proposing. Things were a bit uncomfortable at first as she was not really into the whole sex thing with Mr. Harris but if she failed his class, it could put everything in jeopardy. Her father expected near perfection from Molly when it came to her grades. He would cut off her money if she did not maintain a neat perfect 4.0 GPA. She needed that money from her dad to maintain her lavish lifestyle. Molly reluctantly agreed to what Mr. Harris was proposing and said that she would do whatever he wanted her to do. Mr. Harris got up and went to his door and locked it and closed the blinds to his office. Molly had a feeling that the extra credit was going to begin a lot sooner than what she had expected. She was going to have an encounter with the professor that was going to leave her with a bad taste in her mouth.

Professor Harris came over and gently rubbed her cheek. Her skin felt like a newborn's skin against his wrinkled old hands. Molly presented an element of youth that he found to be quite invigorating. Molly sat there quietly waiting to see what the old man's next move was going to be. Professor Harris took his hand and slipped it under the top that Molly was wearing. He could feel the outline of her erect nipple through the fabric of her Victoria's Secret bra that she was wearing. She had a nice full set of tits for such a young woman. This allowed him to feel young again. Professor Harris took his other hand and slipped it underneath the short skirt that she was wearing. Professor Harris was quick to determine that the young lady was not wearing any panties. The older gentleman began to finger the tight hole of the young student that was sitting in his office. Molly, despite her best efforts, tried to keep from getting worked up, but the simple fact of the matter was that she was becoming more and more aroused as the seconds passed. Little rivers of juices flowed from her crotch and began to trickle down into the seat that she was in at the moment.

Professor Harris could tell that this was getting her very much aroused, and as a result, he suggested that she take her mouth and see if she could pass the oral exam that professor Harris was going to give her. Molly began to unzip the pants of the older professor and saw that he was wearing boxers, this allowed for better, faster access to his long, thick, uncut cock that hung down his thigh and was showing signs of becoming very much aroused. Professor Harris was still working over her cunt. In an effort to help get her a little more interested in the actions that were taking place. Molly began to deep throat the member of the professor and see just how far she was able to take it before her gag reflex kicked in. It did not take long before the cock was all the way down her throat and she soon was fucking the end of his knob with her throat muscles. The sensation was one of the most enjoyable that she had in quite a long time.

Professor Harris began to finger fuck Molly's snatch with his fingers. The intention was to get her worked up to the point that she could not hold out any longer, and had no choice but to finally explode in one wave of passion. Molly was getting close and could feel the muscles in Professor Harris began to tighten. She knew that before long, it was going to be time for him to ejaculate down her throat and send wave after wave of jizz into her stomach. When he was done, Molly nursed on the deflating member until it was drained and was now flaccid as it had been when she first walked in. The rest of the semester was pretty much the same, as every week Molly was fucking her professor for that passing grade. The kick in the ass came at the end of the semester. All of the effort she put out and the many loads of cum later, he still failed her in his class and she had gained nothing.

ABOUT THE AUTHOR

Sage Yarber

Sage Yarber is an emerging erotica author of many erotica kinks and sub-genres. Be sure to check out other books and leave a review if this story got you hot!

Visit my blog at Sage Yarber Blog

Join my newsletter for exclusive Sage Yarber Newsletter

Sign up for Free Stories from Xplicit Press Authors

Xplicit Press Author Updates

Like Xplicit Press on Facebook

Follow Xplicit Press on Twitter

Readers: I want to expand a few of the stories to see where the characters can be explored further. If there are any of the stories that you would like to read more about again, I'd love to hear from you!

Keep In Touch

Sage Yarber

info@sageyarber.com

Shala Breece

Shala Breece is an emerging erotica author of many erotica kinks and sub-genres. Be sure to check out other books and leave a review if this story got you hot!

Visit my blog at Shala Breece Blog

Join my newsletter for exclusive Shala Breece Newsletter

Sign up for Free Stories from Xplicit Press Authors
Xplicit Press Author Updates
Like Xplicit Press on Facebook
Follow Xplicit Press on Twitter

Readers: I want to expand a few of the stories to see where the characters can be explored further. If there are any of the stories that you would like to read more about again, I'd love to hear from you!

Keep In Touch
Shala Breece
info@shalabreece.com